PIGS AT CHRISTMAS

Arlene Dubanevich

Christmas Trees

BRADBURY PRESS   NEW YORK   DEC   1986

OC # 13396029

Bradbury Press
An Affiliate of Macmillan, Inc.
866 Third Avenue, New York, N.Y. 10022
Collier Macmillan Canada, Inc.
Manufactured in the United States of America
10 9 8 7 6 5 4 3 2 1

Library of Congress Cataloging-in-Publication Data   Dubanevich, Arlene. Pigs
at Christmas. Summary: As Christmas approaches and panicking pigs prepare
for their holiday festivities, one little pig wonders nervously if Santa will really
deliver everything as promised. [1. Pigs — Fiction. 2. Christmas —
Fiction. 3. Cartoons and comics] I. Title. PZ7.D8492Ph 1986 [E]
86-6891   ISBN 0-02-733160-1

To J.
my loving and supportive husband